told by
AARON SHEPARD

illustrated by
DAVID WISNIEWSKI

For G.B., S.H., and all who
failed to survive them
—A.S.

For Alexander and Ariana
—D.W.

MASTER MAN

A Tall Tale of Nigeria

HarperCollins*Publishers*

Once there was a man who was *strong.*

When he gathered firewood, he hauled twice as much as anyone else in the village.

When he hunted, he carried home two antelopes at once.

The baby quickly pulled up the bucket and filled his mother's calabash. Then he threw in the bucket and pulled it up once more for Shettu.

Shettu gasped.

By the fence were some large clay pots, each as tall as a man, for storing grain. She helped him climb into one, then set the lid in place.

Shadusa raised the lid a crack, to peek out.

And there, coming into the compound, was **Master Man**, carrying a dead elephant across his shoulders.

As Shadusa watched in terror, Master Man built a huge fire in the fireplace, roasted the elephant, and devoured every bit of it but the bones.

Suddenly he stopped and sniffed.

Wife! I smell a man!

Oh, there's no man here now.

—said the woman.

One passed by while you were gone. That must be what you smell.

Just then they heard a terrible—

The farmers all dropped their hoes and covered their ears.

The farmer asked—

What was that?

That was **Master Man!**

Well, then!

—said the farmer.

You'd better keep running!

And the five farmers fled across the field.

Just then the ground—

—and they all bounced into the air. The porters fell in a heap, all mixed up with their bundles.

The porter asked—

What was that?

That was Master Man!

Then run for your life!

And the ten porters bolted from the path.

Shadusa ran on till he rounded a bend—then he stopped short. There beside the path sat a stranger, and there beside the stranger lay a huge pile of elephant bones.

WHAT'S YOUR HURRY?

—growled the stranger.

Master Man is after me!

—moaned Shadusa.

Master Man lunged, but the stranger tossed Shadusa into a tree. Then the two strong men wrapped themselves around each other and wrestled across the ground.

The noise of the battle nearly deafened Shadusa. The dust choked him. The trembling of the tree nearly shook him down.

As Shadusa watched, the two men struggled to their feet, still clutching each other. Then each gave a mighty leap, and together they rose into the air. Higher and higher they went, till they passed through a cloud and out of sight.

Shadusa waited and waited, but the men never came back down. At last he climbed carefully from the tree, then ran and ran and never stopped till he got home safe and sound. And he never called himself Master Man again.

As for those other two, they're still in the clouds, where they battle on to this day. Of course, they rest whenever they're both worn-out. But sooner or later they start up again, and what a noise they make!

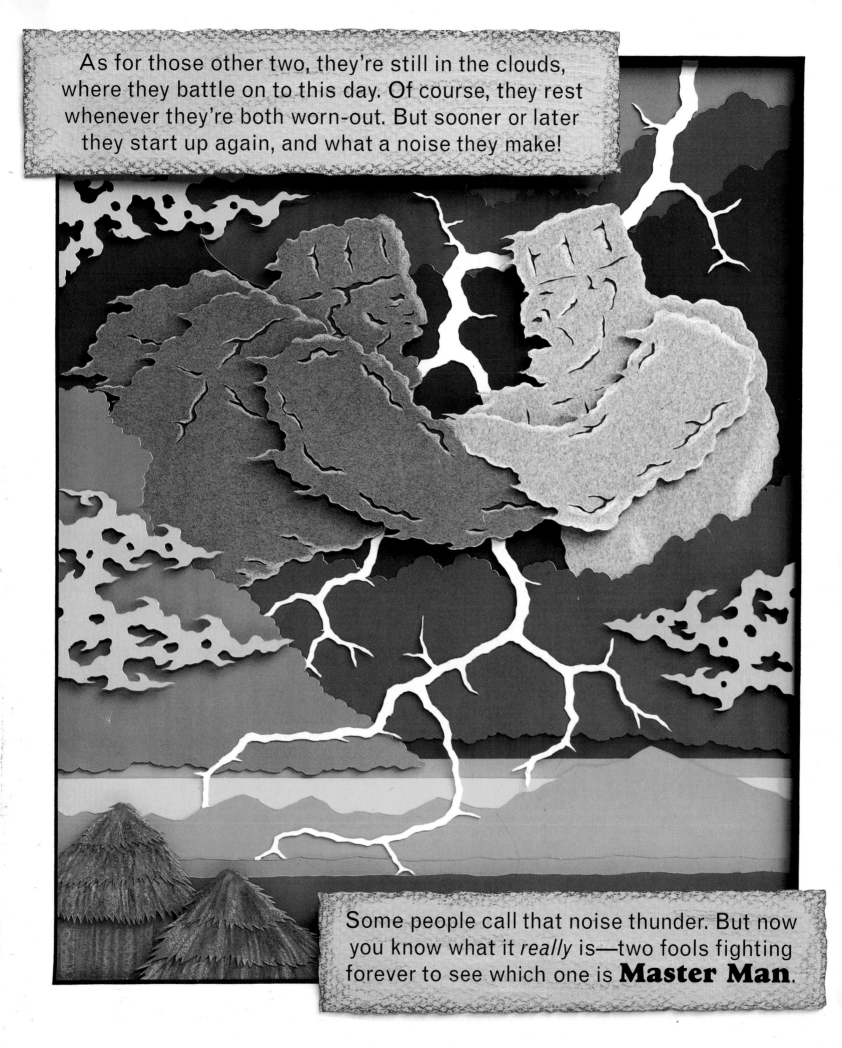

Some people call that noise thunder. But now you know what it *really* is—two fools fighting forever to see which one is **Master Man**.

HOW TO SAY THE NAMES

Shadusa shuh-DOO-suh
Shettu SHET-oo

AUTHOR'S NOTE

"Master Man" is a tale of the Hausa, the largest ethnic group of northern Nigeria. The Hausa live mainly on the savannah (grassland with scattered trees) of Nigeria's northwest quarter.

Though most Hausa live in rural villages—as portrayed in this story—the larger Hausa towns have possessed a sophisticated urban culture since long before European colonization. As traders, the Hausa have for centuries maintained economic and cultural contacts throughout West Africa, and their adoption of Islam led to the early development of literacy and written Hausa literature.

Tall tales about fighting he-men, such as this, are popular among the Hausa. Many such stories feature the stock character Mijin-Maza, or Namji-Mijin-Maza. "Master Man" is my own rendering of this name, which has been translated variously as "A-Man-Among-Men," "Manly-Man," and "Superman."

The main source for my retelling is number 12, "A story about a giant, and the cause of thunder," in *Hausa Folk-Lore, Customs, Proverbs, Etc.*, by R. Sutherland Rattray (Oxford: Clarendon Press, 1913) volume 1. I also drew on several other Hausa variants of the tale, collectively titled "The Story of Manly-Man" and found in volume 2 of *Hausa Tales and Traditions*, by Frank Edgar, edited and translated by Neil Skinner (Madison: University of Wisconsin Press, 1977), which is a translation of Edgar's *Litafi Na Tatsuniyoyi Na Hausa* (Belfast: W. Erskine Mayne, 1911–1913). And I received my first taste of the tale from the delightful "Superman," by Laura Simms, on her tape *Stories: Old as the World, Fresh as the Rain* (Weston Woods, 1981).

For a reader's theater script of this story, visit my home page at
www.aaronshep.com.

Master Man   Text copyright © 2001 by Aaron Shepard   Illustrations copyright © 2001 by David Wisniewski   Printed in the United States of America.
All rights reserved.   www.harperchildrens.com   Library of Congress Cataloging-in-Publication Data   Shepard, Aaron.   Master man: a tall tale of Nigeria / told by Aaron Shepard; illustrated by David Wisniewski.   p.   cm.   Summary: A boastful strong man learns a lesson harder than his muscles when he encounters one of Nigeria's superheroes in this Hausa tale which explains the origin of thunder.   ISBN 0-688-13783-0 (trade)— ISBN 0-688-13784-9 (library)   [1. Folklore—Nigeria. 2. Thunder—Folklore. 3. Tall tales. 4. Cartoons and comics.]   I. Wisniewski, David, ill. II. Title.   PZ8.1.S53945 Mas   2000   398.2'09669'06—dc21   99-48513

1 2 3 4 5 6 7 8 9 10   ❖   First Edition